Spirit Hollow Book One

By

REXI LAKE

Sips & Spells & Wedding Bells: Spirit Hollow Book One

Cover design: Sweet 15 Designs LLC

First Edition: 2019
Second Edition: 2024

Dedication

For Siobhan.

Sometimes the most random things can lead to an idea, but the support and belief from someone that you *can* do the thing makes a world of difference.

For Dixie.

You are the best! Thank you for helping with the little details.

Prologue

Spirit Hollow was exactly how it sounded. A spirit-filled town that sat in a hollowed out valley nestled between the ocean and the rest of northern Maine. The rumor was that the ley lines running under the earth had twisted up when the glaciers were melting and moving along at a snail's pace. As a result, the land of Spirit Hollow was extra magic-infused and so were the people.

Eva was one of those people. At twenty-five, she had been studying magic all her life. From as early as two, the children had their magic bound to prevent any mishaps from occurring. They studied their way through school, learning potions brewing and incantation writing along with science and literature. Some went to college, some chose a career, some stayed, others left, but when the time came for their twenty-fifth birthday, they always returned home.

In the place where it all began, the bindings melted away and the witches and demons who'd spent years learning to harness and respect the magic of the earth were once again granted access to their own unique abilities. That's where Eva was headed. To the church where she'd been bound on her second birthday.

She'd finished up late at the cafe, so she was still in her uniform and apron instead of a comfortable sweater and jeans. She'd been too caught up saying her farewells to the rest of the staff. She wasn't leaving, exactly, but she was taking the graveyard shift for the next year and that meant no shifts at the cafe until her duty to the town ended. At least she'd remembered to grab a jacket on her way out the door. Since the night was coming fast, and the cool autumn air was already frosted with a chill blowing in from the ocean, she would need all the help she could get to keep warm until sunrise.

Dashing into the church just before nine, she skidded to a halt in front of the three town leaders who were present to oversee her Returning.

"You're late," the elder witch said.

The bell in the church tower began to chime and Eva smiled. "I'm right on time," she replied. Thank the ancestors for the bell.

The elder witch hummed in disapproval. But that wasn't anything Eva hadn't heard before. The woman, Mrs. Spritz, happened to be the principal of the high school as well as one of the town leaders. Eva had, unfortunately, more than enough memories of that

stern,
looking-down-her-nose-and-expressing-nonverbal-disappointment-with-her-glare look. Eva was endlessly running just perfectly on time. Never late, but never, ever early. It had earned her the phrase of "Eva Time is on Time" from her classmates. Not that Mrs. Spritz had ever acknowledged that she was, indeed, on time. Nope. Mrs. Spritz had marked her late a solid fifty percent of the time just to prove a point.

"Let's get on with it, Nora. The spirits will be stirring soon." This was from Dr. Goodwin. He'd been Eva's pediatrician when she was a kid.

The last of the council was Mr. Marsh. Eva knew he ran the post office in town, but there was very little else that she knew about him. Which was strange, given how very small Spirit Hollow was. There were only about fifteen hundred residents, so most everyone knew what everyone else's business was.

"Yes, very well," Mrs. Spritz agreed. She gestured to the others and they took their places.

Eva's mother and father stepped forward, flanking their daughter as custom dictated. They clasped their hands around her, forming a small circle.

"On this eve of twenty-five,
your powers from the earth derived,
restored to you in this time,
threads bound in past now untwine."

The five adults spoke in unison, and Eva could feel the magic they invoked crackling in the air around her. She stood still, barely breathing as she felt the harsh brush of ropes tighten briefly around her, then slowly loosen and drop away, like the shedding of a skin that she didn't realize she'd worn.

> *"Earth, Air, Water, Fire,*
> *elements of the high power,*
> *wash away the rope unwound,*
> *restore the magic to the ground."*

A rush of energy swirled around the circle, then pushed inside and the ropes of magic that had bound her dispersed and the sizzling energies soaked into the wooden floorboards.

> *"Spirit come into this place,*
> *reach through distance, time, and space,*
> *embrace your newest charge and guard,*
> *lead her forth into this world."*

A whistling sounded outside the walls and Eva looked toward the windows. In the deepening mist of evening, she could see the rising shapes of her new charges - the spirits of Spirit Hollow were awake.

She let out a soft growl of frustration as she struggled to free her foot from the nearly invisible contraption that her great-great-great-many-more-greats-uncle Bruce had fashioned from some twigs and vines.

“That’s how I caught that bear that was terrorizing the town,” the boastful ghost appeared next to Eva with a giant grin and a smug look.

“That’s fascinating,” she mumbled. “How do I get out of it?”

“Get out of it? Why would you want to do that?” He looked shocked as he asked the question. “The bear didn’t ask how to get out of it.” He huffed in annoyance and disappeared before Eva could say another word.

Of course the *bear* hadn’t asked how to get out of it. It didn’t speak. Eva, on the other hand, was not a bear. Or an animal of any sort. She was a witch having a very difficult night that didn’t seem to be heading towards anything better than the dawn, and the end of her evening.

"Don't worry about him, dear. He's always been on the gruffer side. I think he probably has more in common with that bear than he'd like to admit." The clear voice of her great-grandmother (only one great) Cheryl rang out. "Not to mention, the bear story is really the only story he has, so we humor him."

If Eva didn't know better, she'd swear the ghosts were up to something. Usually she was left alone. The spirits greeted her when they woke, and said good day before they left. Otherwise, they were doing their own thing. Now, she'd counted a dozen ghosts who'd approached her and made more than just a simple greeting.

Bending down, she stopped struggling to pull her foot free or break the noose. Instead, she set her finger against the knot itself and muttered one of the simplest spells she could remember learning - untying a knot. For a brief moment the vines held fast. Then they loosened just enough for Eva to pull the circle from around her foot.

"If Dev was still here, he'd be able to listen to him all night." Eva looked around at the milling spirits as they conversed and did their spirit-ly things. For two months, she and Dev had walked the graveyard, ensured the tombstones were clean of debris, and kept the ghosts of Spirit Hollow in line. Or rather, in the lines.

The graveyard was directly situated in a perfect triangle of three ley lines that crossed beneath the town. The triangle itself was equal on all sides and at all angles, giving the space within it an energy that resonated with the souls of the ancestors. Those who chose to stay, walked the earth each night and had the ability to wield their magic, albeit on a much smaller scale. But while they could do some things, one thing they couldn't do was cross the lines. To do so would not only decimate their soul, it would threaten the balance of power in their bloodline. No one had any knowledge of what might happen if the balance was tampered with. The first and only time a soul had stepped over, the town had lost three witches to a darkness so deep, it had taken three lycans, two demons, and a wandering fae to contain the spells they'd placed on their friends and family. So, to prevent any further ghostly misadventures, or intentional destruction, a minimum of two guards took care to watch the roaming loved ones of the past.

Except, not now. Dev had turned twenty-six, and his shift had ended. No one else was coming of age for another six months, leaving Eva alone.

"Dev is such a good boy," Cheryl said. "He certainly did know how to entertain some of the grouchier ancestors."

Eva sighed. Yeah, she wasn't nearly as good with the ghosts as Dev had been. Maybe it was because she was still new to the job, but she didn't really think so. Dev just had that kind of personality. The kind that people responded to with smiles and greetings and the sharing of stories. Not her. She seemed to have the kind of personality that led to disapproval and disgruntlement from the older generations. And avoidance. Avoidance was something she could absolutely handle. It meant she didn't have to face the disgruntlement. Being a twenty-first century woman with a mind of her own made for some rather disapproving ancestors. But the younger generations had no problems.

And even the grouchiest of elders would smile when she served them their morning coffee.

"I'm sure I can figure it out," Eva said.

"Oh, yes, of course, dear." The worried look on the ghost's face said she didn't really believe that any more than Eva herself did.

Oh, well. Eva didn't have to make friends, she just needed to keep the ghosts in the graveyard.

"Sorry I'm late." A deep voice from behind her had Eva twisting around and stepping right back into the trap she'd just released herself from.

"Mothers and saints!" she muttered, glaring down at her foot, then up, up, *up*, at the intruder.

The overly tall, ruggedly charming, drool-worthy guy hissed in a breath and winced at her expression. "Oops?" he asked.

"Oops?" Eva replied, arching a brow. She rolled her eyes and knelt, muttering the spell to release herself once more. When she was free for the second time, she stood up and put her hands on her hips. "What are you doing here, Lucan?" she asked.

"I'm on graveyard shift with you," he answered, sending her an easy and heart-melting grin.

Eva looked at him skeptically. No way was he telling the truth. He was twenty-nine, well past his year of the shift.

He raised his hands and shrugged. "I guess they didn't want just one person to watch these guys, so they corralled me since I didn't do it."

That brought her up short. "You didn't do it?" she asked.

He shook his head. “Nope. Only full-bloods are required and my year there were already six people rotating the schedule.”

She huffed a sigh. Of course. Lucan was half demon and half lycan. The werewolf half of him negated the clause that required the graveyard shift. Lucky wolf.

“So you’re on graveyard shift with me until Sari turns twenty-five next May?” she asked.

“Yep. Just you and me and our closest three hundred or so ancestors.” He grinned and looked around. “So what do we do?” His eager tone was almost too much.

Eva closed her eyes and silently counted backwards from ten. Then she did it again just to be safe. When she opened her eyes, she found Lucan staring right at her, waiting. “We keep the ghosts in the graveyard,” she said slowly.

“That’s it?” he asked.

“That’s it,” she confirmed.

“Seems like an awful lot of trouble when we could just ask them to stay in it.”

“Except if something goes wrong, no one would be here to alert the town quickly enough to prevent damage.”

“I guess that’s a good point,” Lucan said after a moment of thought.

Eva didn’t bother with a reply this time. Instead, she turned and headed in the direction she’d been going when she’d first been ensnared. While it wasn’t necessary to patrol the perimeter of the lines, it was something to do that kept Eva moving and her blood flowing. Mid-October in Maine, especially right on the coast, wasn't exactly a time of year to spend outside. In fact, it was a time to spend inside. With freshly baked muffins and a warm cup of coffee. These were the kind of days that Eva missed her cafe job. And the warm and welcoming kitchen that always had fresh muffins and coffee.

She missed her fresh muffins and coffee.

She heard the crunch of leaves behind her and knew Lucan was following close behind. They walked the border twice before he spoke.

"Are we just going to walk all night?"

She paused and glanced back at him. "Generally speaking, that's exactly what I do. For one, it keeps me from freezing, and two, it keeps me from falling asleep."

"I could keep you warm if you want to sit down for a bit," he offered.

Eva bit her tongue as the thought of *Lucan* keeping her warm flooded her brain. Yeah, that wasn't going to happen. She shook her head. "I like walking. It gives me exercise." And she really didn't need to be cuddling up with one of the resident wolves.

Small town life was also rumor mill life. And the rumors about Lucan and his pack - literally, the lycan group was called a pack - were that they were a little on the wilder side. Wild was not something Eva wanted in her life. She liked comfortable and cozy. Warm coffee, warm socks, warm muffins - she *really* missed her coffee and muffins - and a routine that kept her solidly secure in what life was about. Wildness was not secure. Therefore, no matter how delicious he looked, Lucan was not an option for keeping warm on a cold night.

Nope.

Not happening.

Ever.

Lucan couldn't keep up with the witch he was serving his shift with. She'd looped the graveyard more times than he had thought any non-shifter could do. Even he couldn't walk in a circle - well, a triangle - for hours on end without being bored out of his mind. But she kept it up. Looking delectably adorable in her long purple coat and boots, she was throwing off every vibe there was to say *stay away.*

Except, he could also scent that little bit of intrigue in her. That I'm-interested-but-I-shouldn't-be glance he'd glimpsed from her when she'd first seen him was what made him pause and observe.

"She's such a good girl, but she's so very modern that most of the ancestors don't know what to think of her," Cheryl said. She'd introduced herself when Lucan had finally stopped looping the yard and settled on top of one of the headstones.

"She has a mind of her own," Lucan replied. He'd seen it on the few occasions he'd crossed her path before. Usually she was running full steam ahead and charging through anything that stood in her way. She'd single-handedly changed the cafe from a simple coffee shop to a full service cafe that served a whole lot more than just the simple coffee that Mike had charged a dollar for in years past.

"Yes, she does," Cheryl's tone was contemplative and thoughtful. Lucan ignored it though and continued to watch the puzzle of a woman that couldn't seem to stay still. Eventually, the ghost drifted away to chat with some of the other spirits.

Dawn slowly approached, and with it a fresh snowfall arrived. The wolf inside him howled in delight at the flakes that drifted through the air. There was nothing better than frolicking in the fresh snow to the beast. It loved the brisk winter weather. Unlike the woman he watched.

"Do you mind if I shift for the last hour?" he called out when she was close enough to hear him.

She paused and looked up at him. After a moment, she shook her head, but didn't speak aloud.

Lucan didn't wait for verbal confirmation. He let the wolf inside burst forth in a brilliance of bright lights of magic and a delighted howl that echoed through the hollow and out over the ocean.

Lucan let the animal play in the snowfall for a short while. After a few minutes of playing, they ran the loop of the graveyard so his wolf would recognize the perimeter from his level as well as the human one. It was important to spend time in both forms in the area to ensure that animal and human were familiar with it. No matter their form, the places would be recognizable.

"So you're a lycan?" One of the elder ghosts asked the question, staring at the wolf along with several others.

"He's half lycan," Eva answered.

The wolf's head turned to regard her. He cocked his head and studied her in the same way Lucan had done. Both man and beast agreed that there was something about her. Neither could identify it though.

Carefully, but confidently, the wolf wound through the tombstones to her side. It bumped against her leg and playfully nuzzled her arm.

"And apparently he's half pet as well," Eva muttered.

The wolf shook its head, sending cold droplets into the air from its fur.

Eva laughed, and the sound made the wolf freeze in astonishment.

Even the ghosts, whose scrutiny had been riveted on the wolf, paused and turned their attention to the clear, pure sound that came from Eva's delight.

"Oh," Cheryl murmured softly. A few ghosts nodded, and Lucan heard as well, but he was fairly sure that Eva hadn't picked up on the sudden change around her.

He bumped against her again, rubbing his head along her arm.

"Okay, okay," she said softly, grinning and finally unwinding her arms to stroke a hand over his fur. "You are a spoiled thing, aren't you?" she asked. The delight and sincerity of her tone had sparked the magic in the graveyard and the blossoming joy of her brought it to life.

She looked up and around her as little stars of magic burst and twinkled in the very air. "Wow," she murmured.

Lucan shifted suddenly, and pulled her around to face him. “You are incredible,” he whispered, cupping her face between his hands.

He gave her the space of a breath to pull away, but when she didn’t and her lips parted in surprise, he gave in to the temptation of her and sealed his lips to hers with a barely contained growl of need and determination.

Uncaring of the audience around them, he took her lips with a ferocity that matched the clawing need that had enveloped him the moment he’d heard her laugh. That beautiful, crystalline, magical sound had ripped through him and turned his world upside down. Now he needed to feel her against him like he needed air to breathe. One hand released her and wrapped around her waist, hauling her the scant inches that separated them and crushing her to him.

“Down, boy!” Bruce called out, interrupting the sizzling moment.

Eva ripped away from him and pressed her hands solidly against his chest, forcing distance when he wanted to eliminate it.

Lucan growled low and tightened his grip on her waist for a moment before he forced himself to release her and step back.

“Go back to your grave, Bruce. It’s almost sunrise,” Lucan said roughly. He rolled his eyes as the ghost responded with a huff and flounced away.

The rest of the ancestors were either staring unabashedly at them, waiting to see what would happen next, or studiously looking elsewhere.

"Oh, for heaven's sake," Cheryl said, floating before them and waving her hands to break the stares. "It's not like you haven't seen people kissing before. Kristian, I know for a fact you used to spy on your neighbors through their bedroom window. And Doris, you were as easy as baking a pie when we were in school. Stop staring and get ready to go to sleep." She let out a dramatic huff and spun around, floating her way toward Lucan and Eva as the others dispersed slowly in the directions of their waiting graves.

"Eva, my dear, we will speak this evening about your magic. I think there may be more to you than we thought." Cheryl spoke warmly, but there was a backhanded compliment in there too. The ease with which it was delivered made Lucan's hackles rise and he wanted to jump to Eva's defense. *He'd* known there was something. The spirits should have known it too.

"Don't growl at me, young man," Cheryl chastised. "I don't mean that she wasn't considered important to me or her family before. I simply meant there is a lot more that we didn't expect." She looked him square in the eye, daring him to refute her. He kept his mouth shut, but he refused to look away. "Now, tomorrow, I expect to see you when I awake as well. No more of this being late nonsense." She turned back to Eva and offered a smile. "Have a good rest, my dear," she murmured. Then she floated away and as the sun's first rays broke the horizon, the few ghosts still aboveground faded to mist and disappeared.

Lucas looked at Eva. She still stood there, stunned and looking both flushed and confused. He held out his hand to her. “Would you like to get some coffee with me?” he asked.

Eva bit her lip, hesitating for a brief moment. Slowly her hand rose and then rested in his. He wrapped his fingers firmly around hers as he pulled her back to his side.

“I don’t know what that was, but I’m looking forward to it happening again,” he murmured roughly. He lifted his free hand and gently tipped her chin up, locking their gazes together. “Many, many more times,” he added.

“Um, I don’t know what I did,” Eva said softly. Her eyes grew wide as she watched the wicked grin spread over his face.

He felt her heartbeat kick up and her breath came faster. He lowered his head and rubbed his lips softly back and forth over hers. When she parted them, he licked his way inside. And when she gasped at the heat he knew she felt from him, he claimed her lips again, drinking in the sound and tasting her as thoroughly as he could with the many layers of clothing that separated their skin.

Eva didn't feel the cold anymore. The snowflakes that drifted against her skin melted fast, leaving only droplets of water behind. Her body was on fire as Lucan's tongue swept inside her mouth and tangled with hers. She didn't know what had led to the sudden reaction, but she couldn't think beyond the next kiss.

It was heaven and hell mixed together inside of her. Ecstasy and need warred until she broke away from him with a soft cry.

"Stop," she murmured harshly, her breath fogging the air between them. Her hands grasped at his arms, clinging and desperately seeking something to ground her from the freefall she'd just experienced.

"What's wrong?" he asked.

She shook her head, unable to answer him. She could hear the rough need in his voice. And she could still feel the way his beard had rubbed against her skin. How his lips had tasted. How the hard length of him had been more than obvious, even through her layers of clothing. She knew he would heat her up. It was why she'd avoided it earlier in the night. But this was more than she could have imagined. This fiery need and swirling lights of magic that had happened inside and outside of her was too much.

"I have to go," she muttered, stepping away from him before she could change her mind. She swung around and took off, walking swiftly toward her apartment and the comfortable, cozy, *empty* bed that was in it. Part of her wished he would follow. But another part, a grateful part, was glad that he didn't.

For the next week, Eva managed to avoid any conversation that extended beyond the simplest of greetings and goodbyes. She told him the first night after their kiss that she needed to think and she needed space. Then she'd walked the graveyard as she always did - alone and thinking. Always thinking.

She caught the occasional whisper of one of the ancestors as she followed her path, sometimes the wind brought more bits of the conversations toward her, but she tuned them out. She was used to being avoided and for the moment, it was helpful to have the solitude.

On the seventh night following the kiss, Eva's peace was broken. Cheryl took it upon herself to join Eva in her path and talk about things that ranged from nonsensical to illuminary. Perfectly understandable for the spirit whose mind was still as sharp as the day she'd breathed her last.

"You haven't taken the time to talk to me about your magic," the spirit said after a long silence.

"Nope," Eva agreed. She had been too focused on what happened with Lucan and had completely forgotten her great-grandmother's directive.

"We need to speak about it. Your magic is -"

"Not very responsive," Eva interrupted. "It never has been. It's just kind of erratic." She shrugged and continued onward.

"No, it's not that. What I was trying to say is that your magic is linked to your voice. You have a Siren's Call."

That brought Eva to a halt. "A what?" she asked, looking at the woman floating just above the ground beside her.

"The Siren's Call is a rare ability that only shows itself in extraordinary witches. Basically, your voice has the ability to influence others, but only when it is intoned with pure emotion."

Eva shook her head. "I've never even heard of that."

Cheryl shrugged. "That doesn't surprise me. It's so rare that the magic hasn't been seen since before I was born. You are probably the first to possess the Call in a century or more."

"So what do I do? How do I control it?"

"You don't. Not really. Your intentions don't control the magic in the same way a regular witch's intentions do. Your magic is directly linked to your emotions and your feelings. That's probably why you make all the ghosts steer clear of you. You don't want to be bothered, and that emotional intent is broadcast on a low level around you. But when you laughed last week? Oh, my stars." Cheryl had a look on her face that Eva could only describe as pure happiness and pride. "Your burst of happiness gave all of us a restful day that was imbued with serenity and cheerfulness. Not a single spirit here could ever recall a peace like that before."

"Oh," Eva managed. Although, she remained skeptical about Cheryl's reasoning. In the months since her magic had been unbound completely, she was barely able to perform the simplest of spells. And there was a lot of emotion behind her intent. Especially when it came to the one she kept trying to use to keep her coffee hot. When she woke up in the early afternoon, she would immediately make her coffee. But with all the running around she was doing, the coffee was usually lukewarm by the time she finished her first cup. All she wanted, desperately, was to keep the life's nectar of caffeine hot. Just a hair's breadth from scalding. Was that really so much to ask?

"So what do I do?" she repeated.

Cheryl shrugged. "Honestly, my dear, I haven't the faintest clue. I've spent the week asking the other ancestors for any knowledge they might have, but all they can tell me is that Rosalia was the last Siren and she's never joined us in the evenings."

"Rosalia?"

"Mmm, yes. Rosalia Fernweather was the last witch with the Siren's Call. Her resting place is on the other side of the church, in a corner of the cemetery that overlooks the water. You might find some information in the library, if you choose to look. But she would be the only one who could give you guidance on your gift."

Eva stared at Cheryl for a moment. "Library research? That's your solution?"

Cheryl shrugged. "It's all I have to give you. I can't tell you what I don't know."

Eva sighed. Okay, that was true. But to drop the tiniest bit of knowledge on a person and then say there's no more info wasn't really the best course of action. At least not to Eva.

She would have to hit the library when she woke up. The one thing about the long, cold nights of her shift, Eva usually was able to fall straight to sleep after a warm bath and crawling under her warm covers. There was little that could be quite so comforting as that.

Cheryl drifted off and Eva resumed her walk. When she reached the corner where Rosalia was supposed to be, she paused and looked closer at the tombstones.

Erikkson.

Jameson.

Frankfurt.

Gentry.

Fernweather.

There it was. Rosalia Fernweather. Beloved wife, mother, friend. 1798-1867. She rested beside her husband Jamie and on her other side was another Fernweather: Jefferson. Her son, perhaps? Eva didn't know, but she did plan to look deeper into Rosalia as soon as she could.

"I wish you were awake to talk to," Eva murmured, her hand resting on the stone just above Rosalia's name. Her tone was soft, but the desire behind her words floated across the graveyard.

"That was really quite rude, young lady." A sharp, unknown voice penetrated Eva's thoughts.

She looked up and gasped at the woman who stood before her. While the other ghosts were filmy and grey, this one was brightly colored and her aura danced with sparkles of magic.

"What?" she asked, staring at the new spirit in awe.

"I said, that was quite rude of you. I don't enjoy being pulled away from my family on the other side simply because someone wants to drag me back over here. We were just about to have our evening tea. The very least you could do is apologize for the interruption."

The woman crossed her arms over her ample bosom and waited. She was shorter than Eva, by at least four inches, and the rather matronly figure seemed to have the same glare that Mrs. Spritz had. Eva almost took a step backward away from the brightly colored apparition.

"I'm sorry. I don't know who you are though," she said.

"You summoned me here and you don't know who I am?" Thick eyebrows rose in surprise.

"I summoned you?" Eva asked. "I didn't summon anyone. I don't even know how to. And my magic doesn't really work like that anyway."

"What is your name?" the ghost demanded.

"Eva. Eva Ronen."

"Well, Eva Ronen. You must be related to those Ronen brothers who came from the south. I'm Rosalia Fernweather. And if you didn't intend to summon me, I would much appreciate it if you released the spell that brought me over and allowed me to return."

"I - what? Release the spell? What spell?" Eva floundered, trying to understand the demands.

"The spell, child. Surely you know what spell you cast just a moment ago," the ghost insisted.

Eva shook her head in denial. "I didn't cast a spell," she insisted in return.

The ghost heaved a sigh and threw her hands into the air in frustration. "I am missing my tea," she complained. "I spent enough years on this earth and I simply wish to rejoin my family on the other side where I am happily living out my afterlife." She began to pace before Eva. Her feet never touched the ground, but she continued the movement of actually lifting her slippers and setting them back down as she floated from one spot to the next and back.

"What was the last thing you said before I appeared?" she asked.

"I just wished for Rosalia - *you* - to be here," Eva explained.

"You *wished* it? That's it?" Rosalia paused and stared hard at Eva.

"That's it," Eva confirmed.

"Heavens and saints above. You're a Siren, aren't you?"

Eva nodded.

Rosalia's brusk demeanor evaporated as quickly as she herself had appeared. "Oh, my dear girl. No wonder your Call summoned me." She motioned to the nearby stone that held her name. "Sit, please. We have much to discuss and the evening will be gone too soon."

Eva sat, waiting silently for some guidance to what this might mean about her magic and her life.

Lucan found Eva in the next town over. He'd given her space for long enough. Now he just wanted to know what the hell was happening in her head. He'd seen her chit-chatting with the weirdly colorful ghost the night before and he'd still kept his distance. But when she took off like a banshee running for the hills, he'd had enough.

What he didn't expect, when he finally tracked her down, was that she'd already be three drinks past tipsy and still going strong.

"What are you doing?" he asked, taking the bar stool next to her.

"Drinking. What are you doing?" she asked in return.

"Looking for you."

Her hand stopped with the glass halfway to her lips again. She set it down slowly and turned her head to look at him.

"Why?"

For a minute, Lucan thought about just shrugging it off and making a joke. But something stopped him from the flippant answer he wanted to give first. Something made him reconsider his own choice of words and the real reason he'd been tracking her down.

"Because I want you," he said truthfully. "We lit up the sky last week with just a kiss in the middle of a snowfall. I was burning up and couldn't focus beyond you and me. And then you changed your tune and brought everything to a halt before it even had a chance to get going. So I want to know why. Because I still want you and I think you still want me too." He hoped that his senses weren't picking up on that hint of desire as a false trail manifested by his own thoughts and desires.

"You want me?" she asked the question slowly. "Are you sure about that?"

He frowned. Of course he was sure. He wouldn't have said so otherwise. "Yes," he answered aloud.

"Careful, you might not be as right as you think you are," she told him. She lifted her drink and took a long swig, finishing the liquid inside. She held up her hand for another and the bartender came over to grab her empty glass.

"What does that mean?" Lucan asked, "Why wouldn't I know my own feelings in this?"

"Oh, well, that might actually be me *wishing* you wanted me and therefore *making* you want me. That's my gift, you see. Emotionally tampering with everyone else's emotions. Good magic there."

Her sarcasm wasn't lost on Lucan, but the bitterness that twisted her tone made his heart ache at the realization that she didn't trust that he had any feelings toward her at all.

"When you were six, you got caught in a bramble bush on the edge of the park and it took three of us to pick out the snags before you could get free."

She looked up in surprise, ignoring the new drink that slid before her.

"When you were fifteen, you were supposed to go to a school dance with Jerry Corshan and he didn't show up. Idiot got sick, but forgot to call you. You went by yourself and spent half the night singing karaoke with your friends at the top of your lungs in a bright blue dress."

Her eyes widened as he spoke, the deep brown depths swirling with something he couldn't name.

"When you went away to college, you swore you were going to run a business one day. Then you came back after a year and decided you didn't want to stay away from town. So you convinced Mike to let you take over running his place. You started small, with just a few muffins and then some sandwiches. By the time anyone figured out what was happening, the cafe was running almost twenty-four-seven and serving three meals a day."

He reached out and pushed the drink back toward the bartender, dropping two twenties next to it. "She won't be needing this one," he said. He stood and held a hand out to the woman whose presence had been there for as long as he could remember, even if she hadn't really looked back at him from where she'd been flying ahead.

"How do you know these things?" she asked.

"Because I'm not confusing your feelings with my own here, Eva. I've been around you since we were kids. Even with four years separating us, you were always just there. Somehow, I was around when you fell into trouble. Or when you were sad. Or determined. Your emotions are yours. And maybe they can influence others if you aren't careful, but you've never influenced me. My desire to be around you was my own. And my wolf's. It still is."

She stared at him for what felt like an eternity. But then she did the one thing he wanted. She placed her hand in his and let him lead her out the door and into his waiting truck. No way was he letting his slightly more than tipsy Siren drive herself home.

It was nearing three in the afternoon when Lucan heard a stirring from the bedroom. A few moments later, a bedraggled and still dazed Eva emerged into the living room. He'd brought her home, tucked her into bed, and then crashed on her couch himself for a few hours of sleep. He'd been awake for nearly two hours, but she had needed more time to sleep off the alcohol fogging her brain.

"Hey there," he murmured as she took a seat on the couch beside him.

"Hi," she said cautiously. She looked around the room, almost inspecting it.

"What are you looking for?" he asked.

"Cameras," she answered.

"Why?"

"Because I'm not sure what you're doing here, or how I got here, or much of anything else right now. And if I'm being hoaxed on some local hijinx show for Halloween, I want to know now before I say or do something I'll later regret."

Lucan laughed. The sound was big and booming, filling the room. "There's no camera up there. We aren't being filmed."

"Then why are you here?" she asked, finally looking at him.

"What do you remember about this morning?" he asked, raising a brow.

"Not much," she admitted grudgingly.

"Well, let's start with this: I found you working your way toward drunk at a bar over in Cliffspring."

She nodded. "I remember going there."

"Okay, that's something. We talked a little and then I drove you home," he said. He waited to see if she might remember what they'd talked about.

"We talked?" she asked carefully.

"Yes."

"Blue dress?" she asked.

"Mmm, that was mentioned." He was surprised to see she did remember.

"I thought that was a dream," she muttered, dropping her face into her hands. After a moment, she slid them up and pushed her hair from her face. "What now?" she asked, facing him.

"Why don't you tell me more about why you felt the need to dive into a beer keg after our shift last night?" he asked.

She shrugged and looked away.

"Hey," Lucan reached out a hand and cupped her cheek, bringing her face back around to his. "What did that ghost say?" he asked.

Eva blew out a breath. It was a few moments before she finally spoke. "She told me that my magic is tied twofold to my emotions. While most of us only have to have their intentions behind a spell, I have to have my emotions behind the intention. And on the flip side, if I have a strong emotion, I might trigger a spell without having to say anything. Just by emotionally willing something and speaking that will aloud, I can do almost anything. If I'm afraid, or scared, I could will away the cause. But if I love or hate, I could will that into being too."

"So when you laughed and the magic stars appeared, that was because you had a pure emotion that pushed your magic out into the air," Lucan reasoned.

She nodded.

"And when you said my feelings might not be my own, that's because you have feelings for me, right?"

She nodded again. Slower this time, but still affirmative.

"You didn't have your magic when we were kids," he said. "Nor did you have it when you served me coffee every morning for the past two years."

His thumb brushed across her lips. "I watched these lips purse in annoyance at a slow pancake order, twist into a frown at a rude customer, and more often than that, they were curved into a smile that lit up the cafe and brought smiles to all your customers daily. And you didn't have your magic then."

"But," she started to speak, but his thumb pressed against her lips, halting the protest before she could voice it in full.

"Your magic is probably going to do things. Probably going to frustrate you along the way. But other than the cold and the graveyard shift pulling you away from your beloved cafe, you normally draw people to you because of the warmth and care you give to others."

She frowned, a look of intense concentration filled her eyes as she listened to his words. After a moment, he lifted his thumb and released her mouth.

"Believe me, Eva. When I say my feelings are my own, it's because they didn't appear over a night watch. Nor even a dozen of them. They've been there for a lot longer than you could know."

"Why didn't you ever say anything?" she asked.

His lips twisted in a half smile, half sneer. "I'm lycan. I may not be a full one, but I'm half and that places me outside of a lot of things. We don't run in the same circles. And my pack isn't generally considered tame by any stretch of the imagination."

Her eyes drifted downward in shame. He wasn't saying anything that wasn't true. When it came to the wolves, most of the townspeople made it clear that they were tolerated, but their wild natures made them less human.

"You never made me feel any less for being lycan," he assured her, following the direction her thoughts had gone. "And many people are better now that there's more mingling of bloodlines."

She glanced up again. That was true. Most of her contemporaries weren't full blooded witches or demons. Many shared other magical bloodlines - like the lycans - now. That was why there was such a space between her birthday and the next witch coming of age.

"So what now?" she asked, hesitantly.

"Now, I still want you," Lucan said.

Eva's heart fluttered, and then her stomach growled. Loudly.

He laughed. "We should probably get some food though, considering it's been hours since either of us ate."

She blushed and nodded.

"Why don't you grab a shower and dress and meet me at the cafe in an hour?" he asked.

She nodded again. "Okay."

"Are you going to show up?" he asked.

She rolled her eyes. "I need to eat, like you said," she answered.

"Are you going to have dinner with me?" he asked, rephrasing.

"Yes," she replied. "Yes, I will have dinner with you."

"Today."

"Yes, today."

"In one hour."

"*Yes,*" she answered, laughing. "Go get yourself ready. I will see you in one hour."

He dipped his head to hers and pressed a brief kiss to her lips and then was gone before she could process the feel of his kiss.

Her fingertips lightly touched her lips, brushing over the spots that tingled with sudden awareness. She stared at the door he'd exited for long moments before finally moving toward the hot shower that was waiting for her.

Ordering her usual hot apple cinnamon pancakes and sausage, along with her coffee and getting slid her special french vanilla creamer should have made Eva feel a little more normal. But there was nothing normal at all about this meal. Not when Lucan was sitting directly across from her and patiently waiting for her to talk to him.

"Eva?" His rough voice sent shivers through her. She blinked at him in return.

"Eva!" He said it a little louder this time and she managed to shake off the frozen-ness of her mind.

"What?" she asked.

"Where was your head?" he asked.

"No where," she muttered quickly, a blush stealing over her face.

His grin widened. "No where?" he repeated, arching a brow.

She shook her head and raised the steaming cup of coffee to her lips. They were sitting in one of the far booths that afforded them a small modicum of privacy. Not that there was really any sort of privacy in a small town. But one could manage to keep the knowledge of others to rumors and guessing games if they tried hard enough.

"After our shift tonight, I want you to come home with me," he told her.

That was what she thought she'd heard the first time, but then her head had gone and dredged up all sorts of things that could mean. Including, but certainly *not* limited to some rather steamy images that she couldn't shake from her thoughts.

"Um, why?" she asked.

"Because, while I would love to have you for dinner instead of the steak I ordered, we need to be at the graveyard for our shift. And I won't have nearly enough time to get my fill before then," he said.

Her eyes grew wide as she heard the truth behind his words. The rough tone of his grew harsher as he spoke, filled with a desire that he barely kept concealed in his otherwise calm demeanor. "Oh." Her lips formed the word, but it was barely a breath of sound that escaped.

"And I have to be home tomorrow for my nephew's birthday," Lucan added.

"Birthday?" Oh dear. That meant a pack event. No way. No way was she going to be introduced to his pack like that. Well, not really introduced. She knew most of them. But still, going to a birthday party for his nephew had all sorts of extra connotations.

"Don't worry, I won't make you go with me for it. You can escape before the toddler terrors arrive." He smiled and rolled his eyes. "You didn't think I would throw you to the wolves that quickly, did you?"

She couldn't stop the giggle that escaped. His description was so literal. "I wasn't sure," she admitted.

He shook his head. "I wouldn't do that."

Their food arrived then and the rest of their meal was spent enjoying the flavors of their dishes and discussing favorite foods, memories of childhood falls, and - as always happens in October - Halloween.

"We'll be on graveyard shift this year, but what do you usually do for the big holiday?" Lucan asked.

Spirit Hollow celebrated the end of October the same way most of the world celebrated Christmas and New Year's. It was their day and night of town-wide celebrations. The day would include kids running around the main street markets, stopping in at the shops for treats, street fair vendors and games would be set up, and everyone would be visiting friends and family. Just before the sun disappeared, the kids would trick or treat around the residences, then they would return to various places for their final parties. Some residents chose to visit the graveyard during the evening and see their relatives that came to visit, but the ghosts usually had their own party going on too.

"Usually I hand out treats at the cafe during the day, then more treats at night in my apartment complex. Since I won't be at either place, I guess I'll get to enjoy the fair a little before going to the graveyard." She shrugged. She enjoyed seeing all the kids. Some of her friends from school already had one or two, and it gave them all a chance to see each other and visit. Stopping at the cafe for lunch or a snack usually meant a brief few minutes to visit and catch up. She wouldn't have that this year. "What do you do?"

Lucan grinned. "I oversee the carnival games."

That surprised her. "I thought you were one of the park rangers?" she asked. Most of the lycan pack took jobs working outdoors. She assumed it had something to do with their wolven side, but had never asked.

"I am." He nodded. "We organize outdoor events for the town as well though. Including the Halloween street fair. My task is usually to oversee the junior packmates running the games. It lets me keep moving around, and since I'm also one of the trainers, it helps the juniors to know and recognize who's in charge of them."

"Oh. I guess I never realized your pack does the events," Eva said softly. It made sense, but she'd never paid attention.

Lucan shrugged. "When you go to one of those things, you're supposed to be having too much fun to pay attention to the stuff behind the scenes. So I'll take that as a compliment."

Eva didn't quite know what to make of that. Lucan really wasn't what she had expected him to be. What happened to being wild? Weren't they - the lycans - supposed to be rough and a little edgy? Instead, she was discovering that he was, well, *tame*. The only thing *rough* about him was turning out to be his voice, his looks, and probably the way he behaved in the bedroom. She was basing that on those kisses of his that had curled her toes and left her aching in ways she'd never felt before.

But the man was revealing himself to be a whole lot more than the rumors portrayed. While she remembered her own memorable events with some accuracy, she'd been taken aback by his recitation of them. If he remembered so much of her, perhaps his feelings weren't being influenced by her own.

That was her biggest fear, thanks to Rosalia. The ghost had talked with her until dawn, when even a Siren's Call couldn't keep her in the physical realm. She'd talked about her own discovery of her gift, and the curse it had brought with it. She'd told Eva about how her fears had led her down a dark path before her husband, the only person who was immune to her Call, brought her back into the light and helped her face and overcome her fears. How she'd spent years working to control her emotions to prevent any misuse of her Call. Before the dawn called her back, she'd cautioned Eva to be wary of anyone who seemed to change overnight. Even unvoiced Calls could be heard if the thoughts and emotions were strong enough.

That had her hesitating. It made her anxious and worried for the people around her. The people she loved dearly and even the ones she knew only in passing. She never wanted to change someone's life. She simply wanted to live her own.

"Eva! I'm glad you're here." Mike, a tall giant of a man came up beside them, pulling Eva's attention away from Lucan.

"What's wrong?" she asked, sensing a problem from the worried expression on Mike's face.

"I forgot to place the order for our coffee on time yesterday, and the guy on the phone is telling me we'll have to wait until Monday to get our delivery!"

"Calm down, Mike." She looked at Lucan as she slid from her seat. "I'm sorry; I'll be back in just a few minutes." His smile and not told her he was fine, and she patted Mike on the arm as she moved past him. She hoped like hell that Mike hadn't made Jeremy too upset. She might need to promise him some fresh muffins for life.

By the time they reached the cemetery for their shift, Lucan was more worked up than he could ever remember being. Eva just had this magnetic pull that made him want her. She glowed. Granted, most everyone glowed to him in some fashion or other. That was the demon side gift - the ability to see auras. But with only half a demon bloodline, his magic wasn't as strong, and it usually took concentration to really focus on someone's presence.

But not with Eva. She just had this golden glow around her that seemed to spread into the people she came in contact with. Like a hug, or warmth, or something. She just was that genuine. Until she was cold. When the Siren felt uncomfortable, she put off this vibe that kept people at bay. Which Lucan found interesting, because it was almost a way of protecting them from her discomfort.

Being cold was, Lucan noticed, the one thing that seemed to deter his witch. And she was his. Even if she wasn't aware of that just yet. He knew it. He didn't know how or when that realization had occurred, but he was convinced they were supposed to be together.

He held her hand for as long as she allowed, but when they reached the church, she withdrew.

"I'm going to walk around and check the older stones. Never know when one might need some maintenance," she added with a slight smile. She pulled away from me before he could reach out and was halfway to the back of the cemetery before he could even react.

Sighing, Lucan took his usual seat on one of the memorial benches that decorated the grounds. Between the number of people buried there, and the number of people who visited, it was almost park-like. Except there were headstones in the field.

Slowly the ghosts woke and began meandering around to visit and talk. Not every ghost came every night, but most came on a fairly regular basis.

"She's different tonight," Cheryl remarked, her wavering form appearing beside Lucan.

"How so?" he asked.

"She feels," Cheryl paused, searching for the right word, "calmer. Less frantic."

"She didn't feel frantic to me. It felt more like fear." He propped his arms on his knees, leaning forward to watch the witch as she cleared some leaves from atop a headstone.

Fear and anxiety was more appropriate, he realized. His Siren was afraid of her gift hurting people. But he knew she would never do that. It wasn't possible. Somehow, her magic had its own ability to warn away people when she was in a place that it might spill over to others in a harmful way.

But would she believe him if he told her? She was still cautious. Still hesitant. But not because she didn't want him. Being half lycan meant Lucan had an extra advantage. He could scent her desire and need. She wanted him as much as he wanted her. She was just afraid that the feelings weren't real. And proving they were wouldn't happen overnight. So he would be patient. As much as possible for a wolf that wanted his mate.

"You should go to her. You're obviously a good influence." Cheryl spoke again.

"No. He should stay away since she doesn't want him around right now," another female ghost jumped in.

"I think Cheryl might be right. She's a lot better tonight than she's been since Dev left. Her keep away feeling isn't as pronounced." This came from a thoughtful older gentleman wearing a tall hat and an eye glass. Closer inspection showed he also boasted a rather prominent mustache and he looked very similar to the Monopoly guy.

Lucan's surprise and curious expression was evident and the man spoke again.

"I fell down some steps after a Halloween party. I made quite the dash at the board game themed bash we had that year." He grinned and tipped his hat.

Lucan shook his head and returned his attention to the rest of the ghosts now gathering around to offer their sagest advice on how to court his witch.

"She needs flowers. You should get her some."

"No, no. Chocolates are best. Flowers wither and die. You don't want her to be sad about dead flowers."

"But she might eat too many chocolates and get a stomach ache. You don't want to make her sick."

"But it's *chocolate*. You can't go wrong with that."

"What if she doesn't like chocolate?"

"Who wouldn't like chocolate?"

"I don't like chocolate. I like vanilla."

"You *are* vanilla. The rest of us like a little flavor for things."

"Are we still talking about candy?"

"No, we're talking about sex."

"Oh. In that case, he should definitely be gentle."

"WOAH!" His voice rose up and he held up his hands.

The bickering group paused and looked at him.

"I do not want or need any advice about sex. I think I can manage to handle that all on my own." He really did not want to hear dead people discussing sex. Not theirs, and certainly not his. That was going way too far.

A soft giggle sounded behind him and he swiveled his head just in time to catch Eva walking past. Great. She had to have heard at least that last bit. He grinned and shrugged. Nothing to do now but ride it out.

She shook her head, but the smile that had been missing just moments ago stayed with her as she kept moving.

"He's smitten."

"Isn't that just adorable?"

"We haven't witnessed a romance in the cemetery in forever."

"Have we ever witnessed one?"

"Probably not. Who falls in love in a cemetery?"

"Not me. I fell in love on the merry-go-round in the park."

"Oh? Were you ten?"

"No. I was nineteen. It was a bit of a whirl, you could say."

"The boy doesn't want or need to hear about your love lives when you had them," this came from Bruce, who moved his way through everyone to plop next to Lucan. "Shoo," he said, waving his hands at the rest of the gathering crowd.

When they dispersed with a few less than polite huffs and glares, Bruce sat back and grinned. "Now, let me give you the real deal about getting your witch. Although, that one is a little pricklier than most. So you'd best be careful how you handle her."

"He won't need to *handle her*, you old demon. She's not an object. She's a person. And a strong-hearted witch too." Cheryl's voice was low, but her tone was nothing like her usual mild voice.

"Hmph." Bruce glared at the woman. "Must be something in your bloodline," he muttered.

"Indeed. It's called intelligence," Cheryl shot back.

"I'm going to take a loop of the place," Lucan said, standing up and moving away from them as they started in on each other.

He started in the opposite direction of Eva, ready to meet her on the far side of the yard and hopefully grab a quick kiss or two. But when he came close to her, she was surrounded by the same trio of women who had first started discussing their living love connections. Veering around them, he avoided the conversation and shot a sympathetic smile at Eva.

By the time the dawn came, and the ghosts departed for their rest, Lucan was feeling wickedly anxious to hold his Siren. She'd stayed just out of reach throughout the night, but her shy side glances and those little waves of lust that he caught scent of told him she was just as anxious for the dawn.

She joined him, approaching slowly, at the entrance and he raised his hand. He wanted her - damn, did he want her - but he wouldn't force the contact.

She laced her fingers with his and he pulled her close, wrapping his free hand in her hair and tipping his head to hers. Their lips met and immediately he felt that pull that woke every part of him and made him ache to possess her. She would be his before the next moonrise. Fully. Utterly. Of that, he had no doubts.

Pulling back, it took him a moment to find his bearings. But eventually he managed to walk her toward his truck. The drive wouldn't be long, but home still felt too far away.

Eva could barely breathe as Lucan drove the truck out of town and toward the small neighborhood bordering the national park that blocked Spirit Hollow off from the rest of the state. The town wasn't exactly secluded, but there was enough of a distance to make it a little insular.

The approaching trees had her heart thudding in expectation. Nervousness mixed with a giddy anxiety and she spent most of the ride trying to keep her heart from beating out of her chest. By the time the rumble of the tires over gravel stopped and the engine was cut off, she was somewhere between ready to run and ready to faint.

Then he pulled her across the seat to straddle his lap in one quick motion that left her more breathless than the ride. Looking down into his hungry gaze, the world seemed to shudder to a grinding halt. Everything disappeared outside of the two of them.

Lucan.

She could feel the hard length of his cock against her thigh. The length of it should have terrified her, but instead the feel of his thick cock made her hotter. Needier. She could feel the slick juices of desire gathering at her core. There was no way he could fuck her in his truck. Not easily.

He came to the same conclusion and wrapped his arms around her. "Hold on tight, little Siren." His words were the only warning before he moved with his lycan speed. Getting them inside the house, he closed the door and spun around to slam her back against it as his lips descended to hers. Eva's sharp inhale was drowned by the growl that reverberated from him and into her very soul.

Her arms tightened around his shoulders and she emitted soft cries that were captured as his lips sealed to hers and his tongue slid along her tongue. Tangling, teasing, tasting. She couldn't get enough and it was all too much at the same time. Eva's heart stuttered and her magic sparked, drawing out the need and desire and turning it into a flaming inferno as his hips ground against hers and the ache became almost unbearable.

"Lucan," she gasped, a soft begging sound, as she tore her lips from his.

He pulled at the zipper of her jeans and when it stuck, he simply grabbed the waistband and tore them open. There was the briefest brush of claws against her skin and she shivered at the sensation. Sharp points, cool and hard, dragging across her flesh with the lightest of caresses. It was delicious and terrifying. The knowledge that he could rip her apart as easily as he had her jeans crossed her mind.

Then his claws were gone and his fingers dipped beneath her panties and the ability to think disappeared.

She shrieked as Lucan slipped two fingers deep inside her core and curled them, finding that spot that made her muscles clamp down hard as pleasure shot through her body, from the toes curling at the wicked sensation to the crackling air above her head where her magic played.

He chuckled roughly, his eyes dancing with a wicked, sinful delight. Then he stroked again. And again.

The endless friction had her trembling. Everything inside her vibrated as those inner muscles milked his fingers and the cascading torture of ecstasy built up into a torrential flood that hit her like a cannonball.

She screamed. Loud and long, as the world first crashed in on her, then expanded until she saw nothing but the stars whose lights were dimmed by the sun's beams.

She felt her magic shift and sharpen before it burst from her in an outpouring of energies. There was no way to hold it back. But even as she realized it, she recognized that the magic wouldn't harm anyone. Sex magic was powerful, but love magic would only affect soul mates.

It couldn't have been more than a few minutes before she slumped against him, her body sapped of any strength. As he gently pulled his fingers from her body, she let out a soft whimper at the loss.

"We aren't done yet," Lucan whispered against her ear. "That was just the appetizer."

She registered the words, but only barely as he carried her to his room. He laid her gently on his bed and pulled the rest of her torn clothing from her flushed body, leaving her naked and utterly open to his gaze.

And he took full advantage of her languidness to look his fill as he pulled his shirt over his head. Eva's eyes drifted over the sculpted abs and chest. He was more than appealing to look at. She wondered if the hair that covered his upper chest and tapered down beneath his jeans was soft or coarse. Her hands itched to find out and her fingers twitched just slightly in response to the thought. He smirked; she knew he could see the hunger in her eyes, though he couldn't possibly know her thoughts. Then his hands went to the button of his jeans. Eva held her breath as the material parted and inched down his hips.

She couldn't hold back the soft gasp as his cock sprang free. He was big. She'd *felt* it against her. But the evidence was more than she could grasp - literally, she didn't think her fingers could wrap around it and touch. He fisted the base as he kicked his jeans aside and approached her.

Standing between Eva's legs, he leaned over, letting the thick, engorged length rest along her soft stomach.

"Don't worry, little Siren. You can take me," he whispered.

Her wide eyes said she didn't believe him. She bit her lip as she shook her head. No, it wasn't possible.

"You can," he insisted. "But we've got some things to do before we get there."

A grin spread wide over his features just before he hooked his arms beneath her knees and pulled her up the bed until his face was just above her pussy.

"That will be dessert. First, I need my dinner."

Eva's eyes widened as he lowered his head and lightly licked along the crease of her thigh. Soft shivers ran along her flesh as he left a hot, wet trail along her skin. He repeated the same on the other side. Then he lifted her legs, placing them over his shoulders, and gripped her hips in his hands. Holding her still, he lowered his head again and sucked her clit between his lips, flicking his tongue back and forth over the sensitive bud. A low moan filled the room as Eva's body trembled from the onslaught of delicious torture.

When he finally released the swollen nub, it was to lick his way down and press his tongue deep into her hot channel. His tongue stabbed into her over and over, teasing with the almost penetration that was enough to taunt but not enough to take her to and over that edge again.

Her eyes fluttered as her vision wavered. The endless waves of pleasure kept her dancing in that place of tense anticipation. He wasn't stopping to let her breathe. He was truly feasting on her like a final meal. His lips and teeth teased across her flesh. His tongue traced circles that made her whimper. She lingered in that space of frustrated desire. Reaching for the pinnacle and never getting close. She begged him through tears that streamed down her cheeks.

Finally he slowed his assault on her senses. He nipped at her inner thigh, hard enough to leave a mark and sharp enough to grab her full attention.

"Are you ready for me, Siren?" he growled.

"Yes! Dammit!" She practically shrieked her reply.

He grinned and slowly crawled his way up her body until his face was over hers and their bodies were aligned.

He felt hot and hard against her. Briefly she wondered if he was real. If anything was real. Or perhaps it was all a very, *very* good dream. Then his lips latched onto her neck and he sucked at the soft, tender flesh. She moaned as the rolling waves of pleasure crashed into her again.

She felt the head of his cock brush against her and she tipped her hips up, anxious to feel it inside her. To feel it stretch her wide and fill her up. Her nails dragged down his sides and settled on his hips, attempting desperately to pull him closer. She needed that penetration. Her body craved it.

"Please, Lucan."

"Almost, Eva," he promised. He reached down and gripped his cock as he slowly pushed the head into her drenched pussy.

She gasped and arched into the contact. The stretching was almost unbearable. He was barely inside her and she already felt full, but still ached for more.

Gently he rocked against her, pushing in and pulling back. Each thrust went a little deeper. The friction as he pulled back and pressed in was deliciously sinful. She'd never felt so full before. The contrasting pain and pleasure rocketed back and forth inside her until she couldn't distinguish one from the other.

It was heaven and hell. Pain and pleasure. Tantalizing and torturous.

"Lucan, please," she begged.

Her body was on fire. Every shift of the air was like ice cold flames licking at her heated skin. The first orgasm had drained her energy, but the one that was building was going to shatter her if she ever reached it.

"Take a deep breath for me, Siren," Lucan said. He balanced himself on his heels and gripped her hips with both hands.

She felt the thick head of his cock still lodged inside of her as he withdrew. As she sucked in a lungful of air, he surged forward, burying the full length of his hot, thick cock deep into her core. She screamed, a guttural cry that spilled into the room as his body claimed hers in one thrust.

Dancing lights filled her view as the world tore apart. She couldn't feel anything beyond their bodies melded together. The very air tasted of magic and as he repeatedly thrust deep and hard, his hips slamming against her thighs, and the wolf inside him claiming her for his own.

"Come for me again, Eva." His fierce growl rumbled over her skin. Her body shook with fierce need as the desire to obey his demand filtered through her pleasure-fogged brain and triggered a series of mini explosions of sensation in her core. Small pops of magic danced along her skin, bubbles that tickled and tantalized and left behind whispers of an electric current that pushed her higher into a stratosphere of need that she'd never reached before.

"Now, Eva," he grunted. His hips slammed against hers. Harder. Faster. She could feel his own desperation dragging through him. The dusting of magic cleared before her eyes and his bright blue gaze met hers with a glowing intensity that demanded her obedience.

Her nails dug into his wrists as she clawed for an anchor to hold onto to no avail. Her lips parted on a silent, aching cry that emanated from deep inside her soul as the tension finally, utterly, snapped. Everything splintered as her body flew apart and her mind expanded until the only remnants of her were linked to a thousand strands that buzzed with euphoria. The core of her glowed bright as the sun and drew together the strands of memory and knowledge that floated in ecstasy. Everything returned in a haze, and she resurfaced to consciousness of where she was. She could feel the howl that echoed through her still and finally, exhaustively, flew from her throat in a keen that was broken up by the sobs that wracked her destroyed essence.

Every part of her was torn asunder. The pleasure that ripped through in a waterfall of painful and euphoric waves left her numb and overly sensitized all at once. It was surreal. A cascade of colors as the fireworks refused to abate enough for her to catch her breath.

Then Lucan's body tensed, and his release joined hers. The mix of pleasure and the outpour of magic from both of them rose up to envelop them in a mix of their essences. His darker red magic mixed into the spaces between the dancing stars of hers until they were surrounded by an enchanted cocoon of desire.

Even as their bodies relaxed and the waves of orgasm melted into a soft glow, the cocoon remained, locking out the rest of the world.

His body lowered over hers and his lips brushed across her cheeks, eyes, brow, before finally settling on her lips. For long moments, they remained locked together. The languid kiss was full of promise. For more time. For more emotion. For more everything.

They stayed tangled together, letting the soft, endless kisses soothe the riotous energies. Their hearts continued to beat in a desperate rhythm and their magic swirled in a cloud of red and white that danced in time to their heartbeats.

It was several hours before they regained control and could rein back the dancing lights. Hours where his cock stayed buried inside her. Hours in which his body stayed pressed to hers. Hours of blissful, sated, beautiful perfection.

Perfection that slowly ended as the world itself faded and sleep claimed them both for the day.

Waking up with Eva in his arms was better than Lucan could have thought possible. He'd been fully prepared for her to disappear on him before he woke, but instead she was still fast asleep, snoring softly, when he returned to consciousness.

After the rather impressive display of fireworks in the early hours of the morning, and the long hours of soft touches and softer kisses, Lucan felt more than satisfied. And definitely a little smug, too. But as he leaned over her to kiss her awake, he was very content to enjoy the feeling of confidence that he had in her and them. She was his now. Nothing would take her away.

The wolf inside him yipped happily in the back of his mind, fully agreeing that this woman – this Siren – was theirs. Their mate.

She moaned softly and came awake slowly as he caressed her body. He couldn't resist the temptation to bring her over the edge again. He played with her clit, teasing her body, and coaxing it into a soft orgasm that rolled through her as she came fully awake.

Pulling her beneath him, her languid body still soft from sleep and drenched with need, he knew it wouldn't take much to fit his cock deep into her snug little pussy. Wolves were well endowed, but it was a lycan secret that their mates would be able to take them without harm to them ever. Still, he was cautious as he pushed between her soft lips and felt her walls stretch to accommodate his girth and length.

She raised her hands to his shoulders and he felt her nails dig into his flesh as she struggled to breathe through the sudden sensations. He lowered his head and nipped lightly at her shoulder, leaving little bite marks along her soft skin.

Pulling out, he heard her whimper and her body trembled beneath his.

"Breathe, Siren," Lucan whispered against her ear. He felt her Inhale and as the breath filled her lungs, he thrust forward, burying himself to the hilt and reveling in the scalding heat of her body as it gripped his cock like a tight fist.

"Lucan!" She was whimpering, her body twisting anxiously, begging for more.

"Hold on, little Siren," he said. It was her only warning before he stopped being soft and let the demand to claim rise up. His teeth dug into her shoulder as he fucked her harder than before. Slamming into her body fast and furiously. The headboard bounced against the wall with such speed, he almost willed it to break. But instead, his sweet Siren screamed out her orgasm as it crashed down on her with a ferocity and suddenness that had him picking up speed to catch up and find his own release with her.

They were both sweaty and sore when the world righted itself once more. She lay on top of him, his hands tangled in her dark locks as she rested her head on his chest. He listened to the sound of her breathing as it slowed from erratic to even and measured. When she let out a soft sigh and her body flowed like liquid into an even softer slumber, he let himself relax and doze as well. There were still plenty of hours in the day before they needed to be awake.

The next time he woke, it was getting close to when his alarm would go off anyway. Lucan snuck from the bed, leaving his pretty Siren mate sleeping while he grabbed a quick shower and then made some coffee and breakfast.

She walked into the kitchen just as he was pulling the last strips of bacon from the griddle. He looked up and grinned at the sight that greeted him. Her hair was still a mess of tangles around her face. Her eyes were still a little soft with sleep. And she was wearing one of his t-shirts that came to just above her knees.

“Coffee is ready and I was just finishing up breakfast,” he told her, still grinning.

"I think the bacon woke me up," she murmured, moving toward the coffee pot. He watched as she carefully poured a cup for herself and added cream and sugar to it. He was glad he'd had some in the house. He didn't use either, but both of his sisters did and they stopped by way too often to not have it in stock.

He turned off the griddle and grabbed the last plate to take to the table. Pausing behind her, he wrapped his free arm around her waist, and pulled her back against his chest. He pressed a kiss to the top of her head. "I'm pretty sure something else woke you up the first time," he murmured.

"Mmmm," she murmured as she took a sip of her coffee. Her eyes closed and he watched as she inhaled the smell like it was the only thing worth doing. After a moment, her eyes opened again and she glanced sideways at him and gave the tiniest smirk. "There was something, I vaguely recall. But I'm not sure how much was a memory and how much was a dream."

"Little witch, I will happily remind you again before we go to the cemetery tonight. But we need to eat and I have a few things I can't get out of today. You're welcome to stay and join me," he offered.

She bit her lip and looked away. "I'm not sure," she murmured.

"There's still time to decide," he told her. "Let's eat breakfast and then we'll figure it out. There's no pressure." As much as he wanted to introduce his mate to his family and pack, she needed to be ready first.

She rubbed at the spot on her shoulder where his mark would be visible if the shirt wasn't covering it. It was an absent-minded gesture that she probably didn't even realize she was making. But it was enough for him to know she was balancing on the edge of indecision.

Gently, he guided her from the kitchen to a seat at the small table in the dining room. "Grab what you want; I made a little bit of everything."

Her wide eyes looked over the contents that covered the table. "Are you always this hungry?" she asked.

"No. But I wasn't sure what you liked to eat, so I made anything I had that was breakfast-y." He shrugged. It was the truth.

"I would have been fine with just coffee," she said.

"You need food, Eva. Not just coffee. Especially after last night." Expending that amount of energy required replenishing it as well.

She blushed and looked down at her coffee. That reminded him that he needed more coffee as well. He brushed another kiss across her hair as he moved past her. He just couldn't resist touching her. It was like his hands couldn't keep to themselves. His first two cups of coffee were already gone and he was still fighting the desire to crawl back into bed. Of course, what he wanted to do in that bed had absolutely nothing to do with sleep and everything to do with the dark-haired Siren sitting in the next room.

When he sat down across from her, a full cup of coffee for himself as well, he saw that she'd added eggs and bacon to her plate. He made a note of that in his head for the future. Then he filled his own plate with a little of everything. He'd made it, so it might as well get eaten. They were almost done eating when his cell phone rang and a knock sounded at the door simultaneously.

Lucan frowned and glanced at the clock. It was too early for the party to start, and even too early for set up, so he had no idea who was interrupting. As Eva raced for the bedroom, with her coffee, he grabbed his cell.

"One moment," he muttered, and opened the door.

"Luc! Thank the spirits you're here." His younger sister threw her arms around his neck in a quick hug before rushing past him into the house.

"Oh good," said a voice over the phone. It was his older sister. "I sent Lessa over early to help you with the cooking. I know you can handle it, but I don't want you doing everything. That's not fair."

"Talia, I have everything under control," he said through gritted teeth. "And I really wish you would have called to check that I wasn't in the middle of something."

"Sorry." He could hear the eyeroll in her tone. "*Were* you in the middle of something?"

"Yes, actually. And she's going to completely freak out on me, thanks to you and Thing 2 who just barged her way inside."

"*She?!"* The screeched question had him pulling the phone away from his ear. Damn it. She knew how much he hated when she used that high-pitched tone.

"Good bye, Talia. I will see you at two to set up the backyard."

"But -." He hung up the phone before she could say anything further, then he closed the door that still stood wide open and went in search of his other pain-in-the-ass-but-he-still-loved-her sister.

"I think I should go," Eva's soft voice came from the stairwell before he could locate Lessa.

He turned to find her still wearing his shirt, but with her jeans back on and her shoes as well. How she'd secured her jeans was beyond him, since he distinctly remembered tearing them from her at dawn.

She'd pulled her hair into a messy ponytail, which made him want to pull it out and see it flying free around her shoulders again. But all in all, she looked ready to walk out the door, which was not something he wanted to see.

"Please don't," he said, walking to her and tipping her chin up to brush a kiss over her lips. "Come finish your coffee and breakfast while I get rid of my sister." He wasn't opposed to begging if he had to. Anything to keep his mate with him for a few more hours.

Eva shook her head. "I don't think I'm ready for the family thing," she said.

He wanted to argue because he wanted his mate to stay. But he wasn't selfish enough to do so. Instead, he nodded. "I get it. My pack can be overwhelming at the best of times. And a birthday party for a four-year-old is not going to be one of those times." He gave her a smile. "Take my truck at least to get to your place. And I'll see you tonight for our shift."

"Okay," she agreed.

He walked her out the front door, grabbing up his keys from the hall table, and then opened the driver's side door. "Be careful," he murmured as he helped her in.

"I won't let anything happen to your truck," she said.

"I meant you," he replied. He stepped up and pressed a hard kiss to her mouth, wishing he could just pull her right back inside. But instead he pulled back after a long moment. "I'll see you tonight," he promised.

"Tonight," she agreed.

He waited until the truck was a few blocks down the road before going back inside the house.

"So, who's the girl?" Lessa asked coyly, holding a slice of bacon in one hand that she was munching on.

Lucan growled and glared in response. "Go do whatever you're here to do while I get dressed." He stalked past her, snatching the bacon from her hand and continuing back to the bedroom and the lingering scent of his mate.

When Eva met Lucan at the gates shortly before the ghosts awoke, he'd pulled her into his arms and kissed her until she could barely think beyond the feel of his body pressed against hers. It was that good. Too good.

When she'd left his home, she'd gone straight to her own place and spent the better part of two hours remembering the night before and wondering just how things had fallen into place so quickly. But he'd managed to convince her that his intentions were genuine. Or, at least, he'd managed to convince her that he'd seen her before the gift showed up. Part of her wondered if that little kernel of interest had bloomed into full attraction because of the gift, but she pushed the thought aside as she rubbed the spot on her shoulder where his teeth had left a rather obvious bruise.

Thankfully it was colder weather and no one would be seeing the mark before it faded away. She would have to be a little more careful once the weather turned warmer. Being marked like that would draw a lot of stares and probably some rather catty remarks. Eva loved the town, but there were definitely some aspects of a small town she would love to avoid - being singled out in the rumor mill was one of those.

"Beware." The warning interrupted her thoughts.

She looked behind her and found Rosalia standing there. "Beware of what?" she asked.

She shook her head, her expression sad and worried. "If he's not your true love, then you're only stealing time. You have to be wary of everyone around you. They may act differently. Or they may not. But your Call will influence everyone you are near. There's nothing you can do to stop it. It simply is. Whatever your emotions, whatever your desires and wishes will imprint on the people here until they are only reflections of your feelings. And then they will start to turn on you. They will haunt you because your magic will turn them into something they aren't."

The ghost stopped. She shook her head and faded a little, but the damage of her words was done. "It's not real?" Eva asked. The words were out before she could pull them back. She didn't want to consider that. She wanted it to be real. To be true. It had to be. *He* had to be.

Rosalia shook her head. "Not likely. No one is ever true. Your gift revealed itself and then he approached you, right?"

Eva nodded, that kernel of dread returning after she'd almost convinced herself there was nothing to worry about. But Rosalia was right. The magic had spilled from her laughter that night and moments later he'd been kissing her like she was the air he needed to breathe.

Oh, spirits! Eva's heart dropped to the ground. How could she have been so utterly stupid? How could she have been so careless? She'd let herself believe in the possibility and now it was false. And worse? She was creating the falsehood.

"Be very wary," Rosalia whispered. Then she faded away like she'd never been there. Eva wanted to wish for her return, but she denied the thought. Rosalia hadn't said anything new. She'd even warned Eva before, at the very beginning. She should have listened. But she didn't.

She looked across the cemetery to where Lucan was roaming with a few of the ghosts greeting him as he passed. He smiled and chatted with them with an ease that Eva only felt when she was in her cafe. But even from a distance, she could see that something troubled him. His smile wasn't quite as big as she'd seen it be. And his eyes kept cutting toward her and then darting away again.

Was that because he didn't understand his feelings? Was it because the feelings were actually just manifestations of her own attraction to him?

Was anything from the past few weeks real?

The fear inside her built into a ball that settled in the pit of her stomach. She felt like throwing up. But that wouldn't make the feeling go away. If anything, it would make her feel more miserable than she already did.

She needed to escape. She needed to put space between herself and everyone around her. But she couldn't do that here. She couldn't even do that in her own home. She would have to leave. Eva sat on the nearest headstone and considered her options. How could she ensure that she was far enough away from people to not affect them? Could she ensure it? Or was it hopeless?

She kept her distance from Lucan for the rest of the night. When dawn approached, Eva fled as fast as she could, not daring to look back to see if he would follow. She had to run, because she'd brought his truck to the cemetery. She'd thought she would be in it with him, but instead, she was running scared. No, she was terrified. She wanted to find her mother and beg to have her magic bound again. But it wasn't as easy to do that. Binding an adult's gift was almost impossible when it was still new and the powers were fluctuating in strength.

She wanted to head to the cafe and eat her weight in freshly baked muffins. But that would put her in contact with others. And in the mood she was in, that could be dangerous for them. She just didn't know.

So she ran home. She locked the door behind her and found her way through the still darkened rooms to the couch. Collapsing onto it, she grabbed the blanket that she used to keep warm while watching television. Kicking off her shoes and curling up, Eva wished for sleep and stared sightlessly into the darkness around her.

She couldn't go back outside. She couldn't be around people. She couldn't be around *him*. Soft tears trickled from her eyes and rolled silently down her cheeks.

It wasn't a gift. The Call was a curse.

Eva buried her face in her hands, wishing she could block the magic from escaping as easily as she could block her own sight.

Lucan paced in front of the gates, barely paying any mind to the restless and wandering spirits that had woken from their daydreams in agitation. Eva hadn't shown up for their shift. And after the way she'd taken off that dawn, he had a bad feeling that there was something he was missing. Something big.

"She's still not here?" Cheryl asked, coming as close as she dared to the edge of the cemetery.

He looked over and shook his head. "No. And I haven't seen her all day either. Whatever happened last night, has her good and scared. She flew out of here like she was on a broomstick instead of her own two feet."

"She was talking to Rosalia last eve," the ghost said. "I don't know much about the spirit or the woman she was, but there were lots of rumors and whispers I heard growing up about a Siren who was unstable. I didn't think about it when I mentioned her to Eva. Perhaps Rosalia was the wrong ghost to speak with?" she pondered.

“Let’s find out,” Lucan growled, wondering just what the ghost had said to his mate. He spun on his heel and stomped to the far edge of the cemetery where Rosalia and her family rested.

He stopped when he reached the headstones. For all his intentions of speaking with the spirit, he had no idea how to do so. She wasn’t there, so how did he get her onto his side?

“Rosalia?” he called, wondering if ghosts could hear through the veil.

Cheryl drifted over and cleared her throat. Lucan arched a brow in her direction.

She smiled. “Would you like some help?” she asked.

He gestured for her to try and waited to see if anything happened.

He probably should have expected it, but the woman blinking out of existence in front of him was a little more startling than it should have been.

Of course, he realized. She was going to Rosalia to bring her back. That made more sense than him yelling into the air at a tombstone.

It was long minutes, almost a full half hour, before Cheryl returned. But it wasn’t Rosalia that she brought with her. It was a tall, lanky boy of maybe sixteen. His hands were shoved into the pockets of a pair of well-worn trousers that had singe marks on them.

"This is Jefferson, Rosalia's son. He has something to share with you." Cheryl nodded at the boy.

Jefferson glanced up and Lucan could see an apology in his eyes already. *Fuck*. The curse slipped through his thoughts. He wasn't sure he wanted to know what the kid would tell him, but he had no choice. This was for Eva.

"Mother isn't supposed to come on this side because she's been a little strange ever since she lost my baby sister. It was an accident. My sister was playing and fell from a tree. Broke her neck in the fall." Jefferson motioned to the smaller headstone that rested on the other side of his father's grave. "But Mother changed. She turned dark and scary. It wasn't until she killed us all in a fire that anyone really knew just how bad her mind had turned."

"What does that have to do with Eva?" Lucan asked, frowning. The kid's story was sad, sure, but it still didn't explain what she'd done or said to Eva.

"Mother's rantings, especially since her own death, have focused on her magic being bad and making everyone around her bad as a result. She's convinced herself that it was her magic that was at fault, not herself and her grief. I don't know what she told the new Siren, but I'm sure it wasn't anything good." Jefferson shrugged helplessly. "I tried to ask her, but she's shut down again. My father and

I do our best to keep her locked in a place that keeps her calm and soothed, but we couldn't prevent the Call that brought her over here."

"So you're saying Rosalia has convinced Eva that her magic is bad?" Lucan asked. That was so far from the truth, he couldn't help but wonder how Eva could believe that.

"Not just bad. She probably told her about the magic influencing everyone to be bad as well. Mother's delusions have her convinced that Ellen wasn't killed in an accident. She was killed by the townspeople that Mother influenced into being destructive because she was mad at my sister when the accident happened. I wish I could explain it better, but Mother's ranting isn't always coherent. Her head is really messed up."

"Wouldn't seeing your sister on the other side fix that?" I asked.

Jefferson shook his head. "Ellen isn't here. Her spirit was reborn a few decades back. She couldn't handle Mother."

"How long ago?" Lucan asked, his thoughts grasping at a singular possibility.

He shrugged. "Twenty-five years or so."

"Eva is Ellen." Cheryl's quiet, awed, statement echoed through Lucan's own head.

He nodded, acknowledging the same thought. "If so, that would explain her believing the woman so readily. She's spent centuries listening to her."

"If she is Ellen, I hope you can save her spirit in this lifetime. She was a very sunny child. But bold. And in my time, women who were bold weren't good." The spirit looked sad as he spoke. "Ellen was more than good though. She could make every person she spoke to feel better about life. It's what I miss the most about her. She was like a fresh sea breeze after a wicked storm. Bold and new and refreshing. She just could make anyone smile." He shrugged. "She should have lived longer, but it wasn't her time."

"Well, *now* is her time. And I'm not going to let some disturbed old ghost ruin my great-granddaughter's happiness and brightness." Cheryl said. She crossed her arms and looked at Lucan with determination. "And I'm pretty sure the reason we're all so disquieted tonight is because her presence is absent."

Lucan had to agree. The anxious energy that had him vibrating with a frenzied desire to run was strange and unsettling at best. While he didn't think it was a result of Eva's fears, he did believe it was his connection to his mate that had him anxious. The wolf inside him felt the same. Their mate was upset and hurting and that just wasn't acceptable.

"Go to her. I'll patrol the restless spirits here. We're all on edge though. Eva's magic isn't bad, but her serene and calming nature help balance the rest of us. Without her, we aren't nearly as stable. She's terrified right now, and that's going to harm her. Living in fear will only make it worse. She needs to embrace her gift, not let it control her. And she needs to do it now." Cheryl's urgent tone had him turning and running for his truck.

"Just shift and run, Lucan," she grumbled.

Oh, right. He shifted from one stride to the next and allowed his wolf free rein to run to his mate. She needed them and Lucan was damned if he didn't want to bring her back from the edge she was tumbling towards.

"Eva! Open the door!" Lucan's voice echoed through the whirlwind that swirled around Eva as she sat in the midst of her living room.

She had tried to hold in the emotional upheaval that had gained traction in the last several hours. She'd even attempted to bind herself.

But instead of collapsing the magic back into its space inside her, it had only grown wilder. The desperation and incredible turmoil was no longer ripping Eva to shreds from within. It was howling in a cyclone that had her trapped. Bruises and cuts along her arms evidenced her attempts to leave the circle, but the angry winds had picked up various items, turning them into shrapnel that was as dangerous as any bullet.

Then she heard Lucan and her fear multiplied. He was too close. He would be hurt. He needed to stay on the other side of that door or whatever was driving her magic into this fierce energy vortex would affect him too.

“Go away,” she shouted above the winds. Tears gathered in her eyes as she waited to see if he would listen.

Instead, the door burst open, slamming back against the wall and Lucan’s lycanthrope demon form - a large wolven creature with glowing red eyes and bulging muscles stood there. Anytime Eva had seen the lycanthropes, she recalled the Hulk movie. Even the little lycans liked to call it “Hulking out” because of the resemblance in the transition. But she’d never seen a demon mixed in. While full-blooded demons, like witches, didn’t have any visible transitions to their form, their magic sometimes brightened their eyes or the aura around them when they utilized it. Lucan’s third form was terrifying and yet she desperately wanted to crawl to him and let him hold her. He could block the flying dishes, the slivers of wood that had once been an end table, and the candles - which had been lit, but no longer - that swirled through the air.

“What the hell, Eva?” Lucan’s voice was rougher than usual. Deep and growly like the beast he was.

She looked at him through her tears. “I can’t stop it,” she whispered. She doubted he could even hear her, but her energy was draining away quickly. Soon she wouldn’t be able to contain the winds and she’d do exactly as Rosalia had warned. She would hurt the people she loved and cared for. She would hurt the town. And everything would be destroyed because of her magic.

“You can stop it,” he growled.

As she watched, he took a step forward. He snagged the bigger items from the air as they passed him by, setting them beyond the wind's grasp. Her eyes widened as he walked through the storm like it didn't exist and fell to his knees before her.

"How did you do that?" she asked.

"Your magic doesn't touch anyone but you when you're upset," he whispered. One clawed, furred hand reached out and cupped her chin. "The winds went around me instead of hitting me because you have no desire to inflict harm on others."

"But I don't have control," she insisted.

"Little Siren, you absolutely have control. But you've been told so many things by a spirit whose mind isn't whole anymore that you've forgotten the basic principle behind your gift and magic in general." His red eyes and furred figure slowly transitioned back until he was human again. "Magic requires intent. And your gift, above others, requires emotional intent. With no intention of hurting others, your magic won't do it. Even when you're sad or angry, you don't pass that on."

"How do you know?" she asked, praying to the heavens that he wasn't lying to her.

"Because my gift is seeing auras and magic even when others can't. It's a second sight, but without the ability to see through time. And you, sweet witch, give off a very distinct 'stay away' vibe when you are unhappy. People steer clear and you don't even have the chance for your magic to rub off on others."

His thumb stroked over her cheek, wiping away the tear trails left there. She sniffled and looked around at the spinning tornado that, despite some distraction, still remained only around her.

"I do?" she asked, looking up into his face.

"Yeah, babe. You aren't going to hurt anyone but yourself with your fears. And that's what this is." He motioned to the wall of wind. "You were fed misinformation by someone who has her own issues and problems. Her gift was a curse, but not because of the magic. It was because of the person holding it."

Eva frowned. She hadn't picked up on that from Rosalia. Could Lucan be wrong? Maybe she was infecting him with her magic and he didn't know it. But he hadn't been hurt. So, maybe he was right?

She closed her eyes as the questions inside her battled back and forth. Believing Lucan would mean disbelieving the spirit who'd shared her gift. But then again, Rosalia had called it a curse and no one else did. A Siren was supposed to be a pure-hearted witch. One whose gift would be used to help heal the spirits of those both living and wandering.

She took a breath and opened her eyes. "What do I do?" she asked.

"Stop being afraid," he answered.

She bit her lip and looked away. That wasn't so easy. "I don't know how," she told him.

His hand tipped her chin back up and his lips found hers. "I do," he whispered against them. Then he claimed her mouth and stole her breath with a kiss that scorched through her fears and burned them to the ground.

As she leaned into his kiss, she heard the clattering of her possessions hitting the floor. The winds slowed and the howling stopped, and when he pulled back, she finally felt the ground beneath her again.

She looked around, noting the mess that was left behind. The air still shimmered with remnants of the magic that had kept her trapped in her home for the day and night. But instead of threatening, it felt refreshing. Like the air after a rainstorm. Clean. Clear. Breathable.

"How did you know?" she asked, looking back at him.

He stood and pulled her up with him. Brushing his hand over a dark bruise on her arm, he took a moment to check her injuries before he answered. Nothing was horrible. The worst were bruises on her arms, a few shallow cuts as well. When he finished, he met her gaze and rubbed his thumb over the spot where his mark remained visible on her shoulder.

"You're my mate, Eva." He spoke with such conviction, she couldn't doubt his words. "Like wolves in the wild, lycans mate for life. And there has never been a bad mating. But lycans whose innate personality is twisted or corrupt don't find their mates. They don't have the capacity to be emotionally attached to anyone. There was no way you could be harmful to anyone, especially if you're a lycan mate."

"Oh." Her mouth dropped. She hadn't considered that there was more than she knew behind his interest. She'd never even thought about the possibility of a mate. She'd heard about them, but she didn't know the logistics of how that worked.

"So, even if my magic had nothing to do with seeing how yours worked, I would know. You don't have the capacity to hurt others. You're too busy making them smile."

She blushed at his words. She liked that he saw that, even though it hadn't been very evident in the cemetery. But really, how could it when she was so cold?

"Do you think you are up to go finish our shift?" he asked, brushing a strand of her hair back behind her ear.

"Our shift?" She looked toward the window and saw that it was nighttime. "Oh no! What are we both doing here? We need to be at the cemetery. What if something happens?" she pulled away from Lucan and searched frantically for her shoes.

"Slow down, little Siren. Cheryl is keeping the spirits calm. They were restless tonight and I think it was your absence."

"My absence?" She located her shoes and pulled them on. She caught sight of herself in a mirror as she stood and winced. She looked like she'd been through a tornado with a dozen feral cats clawing at her. The description was half right, she thought. "I need to at least wash my face," she muttered, turning to walk down the short hallway to the bathroom. She knew he followed, but she was focused on washing the tears from her cheeks and the blood from her cuts.

"Even if you don't realize it, when you're around, people tend to be a little calmer and more level-headed. There's this warmth that you have that just is there, even when you're cold and cranky, you still bring that ray of sunshine with you." He leaned against the door and watched her.

"I do?"

He nodded. "You've never even noticed it, have you? That people smile more after they see you for their breakfast or coffee."

She shrugged. "I feed and caffeinate them, so of course they're happier."

He shook his head. "It's more than that, babe. It's *you.*"

She frowned, but didn't contradict him. She didn't know. She didn't know to look for it either. She really just needed some solid information about the Siren's Call. But there was no one to give it to her. And she didn't want to stumble into another Rosalia.

"Let's go," she said. "I don't want to get in trouble for us not being on our shift."

They reached the cemetery and found Cheryl and the other spirits were waiting for them just inside the gates.

"Oh thank the heavens," Cheryl said, approaching Eva and Lucan. "Now, do you two think you can manage to finish your shifts without any other problems?"

Eva raised her brows. "None of this was intentional," she murmured.

"Well, maybe not what happened in between," Cheryl admitted. "But this -" she motioned with a finger between the couple, "- was absolutely intentional. Why do you think I recommended Lucan be pulled on duty with you?"

"*You* recommended it?" Lucan asked, frowning.

"Well, of course. Nora and I had a good long chat about what to do when Dev's shift ended and Eva was on her own. She mentioned that she knew you two were mates and I thought this would be a great time to put you together."

"*Mrs. Spritz* said that?" Eva sputtered.

Cheryl blinked. "Well, of course. She would know better than anyone. She's a Cupid."

Epilogue

Four Months Later

"I cannot believe you're getting married today. I never thought you'd settle down so quickly." Eva's mother helped secure her veil in place as she spoke. "Then again, your father and I were fairly fast to do this as well when we were your age."

"You told me it was love at first sight for you two," Eva said with a smile.

"Well, it was. Although, if it wasn't for Nora Spritz sending me on a wild demon hunt for some silly book, I don't know if we'd have crossed paths so quickly."

"What do you mean?" Eva frowned, turning from the mirror to look at her mother directly.

"Oh, well, before your father and I bought the antique store, he just worked there and I had a job in the school library. Nora called me looking for a rare volume from some obscure writer. I don't even recall the name or title now. But your father was still new in town and when I went looking for old Mr. Lonzer, I found him instead."

Eva's mother paused mid-smile and looked thoughtful. "Actually, now that I'm thinking about it, I don't remember ever finding the book for Nora. I should ask her about it next time I see her. She may still be looking for a copy."

Eva watched in shock as her mother turned away and gathered up the two bouquets that sat on the table nearby. Great-grandma Cheryl hadn't said Mrs. Spritz made it a habit of matching people. But apparently, that was the case.

Taking her flowers from her mother, Eva pushed the thoughts from her head. Mrs. Spritz could be thanked for a number of things, but for the evening, there was no one Eva wanted to think about more than the man waiting for her on the other side of the church doors.

"Are you ready?" her mother asked.

"Very," Eva answered.

She watched as the doors opened into the night and the dark path to where her future husband waited was lined with the dancing lights of her magic and the glowing forms of the town's spirits. They'd chosen the cemetery at midnight for their wedding. It was the place they'd met and seen each other fully for the first time. And it was the ghosts that roamed that had inevitably brought them together.

Halfway down the aisle, on her right, Rosalia stood looking sad and forlorn.

"I'm sorry," the ghost whispered.

Eva paused and offered the long dead woman a smile. Lucan had confided in her that he believed she was the reborn spirit of Rosalia's daughter Ellen. To lose a child must be devastating. Eva couldn't hold onto any anger toward the spirit. It just wasn't in her nature.

"You're forgiven," Eva answered. She let the warmth inside her, the light that sparked her Siren's Call, expand and flow from her and over the crowd of living and wandering spirits. It was a joy to share her joy with these people. Her family by blood and by history.

She resumed her walk and turned her attention to the man waiting patiently for her. She didn't remember much of the ceremony itself. She knew she spoke words of affirmation and love. She recited her vows without pause. But it wasn't until the end that she became truly aware of her surroundings.

"You may kiss your bride," the priest said.

Lucan pulled Eva into his arms and lowered his lips to hers for the kiss that would seal them together. She already wore his mark on her shoulder. Now she would wear his ring on her finger.

As the bells in the tower rang out the midnight chimes, the guests cheered the joining of two of their own.

The End

Letter From The Author

Dear Reader,

I hope you enjoyed your trip to Spirit Hollow. This was a fun story to write after a rather interesting Facebook post that led to a conversation about haunted cemeteries. So many possibilities have emerged from this silly conversation and I cannot wait to return to Spirit Hollow with you again.

If you enjoyed the story, I do hope you'll leave a review and let others know about it.

Thank you,

-Rexi

About The Author

Rexi Lake is a dreamer. Trapped in the mountains of Western Pennsylvania, she travels to worlds that exist in her head. When she emerges from the clouds a little bit, she shares the stories of her characters' lives with others. Rexi has always believed that the world deserves more happlly ever afters, so she brings them into the world the best way she knows how: through her words.

Recently, Rexi has branched out in her stories to include two new pen names. Under the Rebel Love name, Rexi dives into darker themes and the world of motorcycle club romances. Trigger warnings accompany each book under this name. Read with caution and awareness. And as Raina Lake she co-writes middle grade fantasy adventures with her daughter, Naya Lake. These books are fun, adventurous, and entertaining.

You can find Rexi on a variety of social media sites, as well as her website. She does her best to attend 2-4 author events each year. Follow her for more information on upcoming releases and appearances. Just search @RexiLake on Facebook, TikTok, or Instagram to connect!

Other Novels by Rexi Lake

Just Say Yes World (Reading Order)

Claimed by Christmas (Claimed #1)

Claimed in Cuffs (Claimed #2)

Claimed in Chains (Claimed #3)

Claimed by the Chef: Turn Up the Heat (Claimed #4)

The World of the Imagi (Reading Order)

For the Love of Coffee (Fated Mates #1)

For the Love of Chocolate (Fated Mates #2)

Mistletoe Magic (Fated Mates #2.5)

Eric's Eternity (Eternal Steel #0.5)

A Magickal Christmas Gift (Fated Mates #2.7/True Heart #0.5)
Re-release

Fairyfales

Wicked for Him #1

Being Her Beast #2

Spirit Hollow

Sips & Spells & Wedding Bells #1

Herbs & Howls & Wedding Vows #2

Standalones

Keeping His Kitten (Leather Persuasion Multi-Author Series)

Securing His Star (Leather Persuasion Multi-Author Series)

The Lady of the Lake (Loch Gaoil Multi-Author Series)

Sweet Cider Sin (Bad Apples Multi-Author Series)

His Guiding Light (Forever Safe Christmas II)

His Christmas Rose (Forever Safe: The Twelve Days of Christmas)

The Hitman's Fall *Re-release*

Anthologies

Eternal Steel Beginnings (Hearts of Steel Charity Anthology) *Original Version of Eric's Eternity*

The Hitman's Fall (Heart of an Alpha Charity Anthology) *Original Release*

A Magickal Christmas Gift (A Small Town Christmas Charity Anthology) *Original Release*

Every Princess Deserves Fairy Lights & Booty Rubs (Flirty in Kansas City 2022 Anthology) *Original Release*

Just One Night (Cuffs & Cuddles Anthology) *Original Release*

The Dragon's Match (Flirty in Kansas City 2024 Anthology) *Original Release*

The Bunny's Match (Dreaming Dirty in Michigan 2024 Anthology)
Original Release
The Alpha's Matches (Dreaming Dirty in Maryland 2024 Anthology)
Original Release

**Note: All Anthologies were released for a limited time. The stories in each are released as individual books once the limited time has passed. Re-released stories are noted only if they are identical to the anthology piece. If the story was significantly altered, it is noted under the anthologies as an "Original Version" and not listed as a "Re-release."

<u>Writing as Rebel Love</u>

Sin: Angels and Demons Book 1
Vicious: Angels and Demons Book 2

Turn the page for a sneak peek at the first chapter of:

HERBS & HOWLS & Wedding Vows

Chapter One

Willow smiled as she finished ringing up Selena Cole's monthly order of witch's brew tea. Over the past three years since she had taken over managing Spirit Hollow Apothecary, Willow had gradually introduced several new lines of items for the townspeople. In addition to carrying the usual herbs, balms, tinctures, and made-to-order items, they now carried teas, lotions, bath salts, and other premade goods that were for general ailments rather than specific ones.

Selena, like many of the other witches in town, had a deep love of teas and while many people frequented the coffee shop down the street for their coffees and pastries, the apothecary was where they shopped for the leaves to brew their teas at home. When Willow had suggested the additional items to Helena, the older witch had smiled and told Willow that if her magic felt compelled to offer something new, she should follow that call.

At twenty-five, when Willow's powers had been unbound, she'd found out quick that her magic was *not* that of a Cupid. Her mother and grandmother had smiled tightly, but she could see the disappointment in their eyes. Her mother in particular had always had a difficult time understanding Willow, but now they were practically strangers. Her father and brother had stepped in when her mother had stepped back. Gerald Spritz was a gifted teacher, but his magic was minor, having a small ability to sense strong emotions. It was helpful when the students he taught were feeling overwhelmed by something, and for Willow it meant she had someone to give her a hug when her emotions grew too large.

Kaden, her brother, had the coolest magic she'd seen. As a Flame demon, he had the ability to call forth fire and to recall it. Lighting candles for her birthday cake had been plenty impressive to a seventeen-year-old when he'd first mastered his magic. Now he served on the fire department, as well as being an EMT. And while he was gifted her mother's smiles and praise, Willow worked in her gardens, still getting dirty, and in the small but sunny apothecary.

The little bell on the front door rang out as another customer entered. Having that alert allowed Willow the freedom to be in the backroom when the shop was empty and emerge only when a customer needed her. Putting aside the small bottle of rose oil that she had been about to uncap, she grabbed her journal and went to the front counter.

"Welcome to the Apothecary, what ails you today?" she asked, smoothing open the small book to the next page. It was in her journal that she kept all the orders for her customers, as well as the specific recipes she used for each of them.

She looked up, and up some more, until her eyes met those of Mason Wolfe. Her jaw went slack in surprise, her lips parting on a soft breath of air.

"Hello, Willow," he greeted, smiling down at her from the towering six foot seven inch height that he'd achieved before graduating high school.

"Mason," she returned, her lips quirking into a wry smile. "I didn't know you were coming back into town."

He shrugged and picked up one of the bagged tea leaf blends sitting on the counter. He turned it over and read the back before settling it back down. "Still got dirt on your face, munchkin," he told her.

She groaned. "Will you *please* stop calling me that? It's been a dozen years or more and I'm not the shortest person you know any longer."

"Actually, *munchkin*, I think you might be, at least of the adults." He grinned. "But you do still have dirt on your face." He quirked a brow at her and reached across the counter to wipe his thumb across her cheek.

She laughed and shook her head, moving out of his reach. "I was working on mixing up the latest batch of aromatherapy candles for next month's Winter Wonders sale."

"It's not even Halloween yet, Will. Why are you having a winter sale in November?"

She closed her journal and came around the counter. "You know good and well that we have to be ready for Christmas by November first. It's how shops work. With the online business I have to be ready for those orders to ship out *and* get to my customers before December and Christmas hit."

Mason stepped toward her and pulled her into a big hug. His towering frame and overwhelmingly large muscles made her short and curvy self feel very small in comparison. But that was Mason. Her best friend and avid partner in crime from the time they had met in elementary school.

She'd been the smallest first grader and for some reason, a number of the older boys had thought it would be amusing to tease the little girl she'd been. Mason had stepped into the space between her and the others. Already about a foot taller than her, he'd faced the other boys and told them they needed to back off or he'd bite them and turn them into wolves himself.

Magical children and shifter children hadn't intermingled much back then. None of them knew that getting bit by a werewolf, especially a nine-year-old one, was not going to push them through a change. But the threat worked well enough and the other boys had scattered. That day, Willow had gained a best friend and a protector. At the time, she hadn't understood much about the Alpha-to-be's nature, he'd simply been the boy who made the mean ones go away.

By the time she reached high school, his over-protectiveness had become overbearing. They'd fought more often than not, but in the end he was the one who would show up with her favorite blueberry ice cream and listen to her cry about each breakup. He had somehow managed to outdo her brother on the fiercely protective scale, which still managed to piss her brother off. But with Kaden being eight years older, he'd had much less time for his younger sister. Especially as he went into adulthood as she was still navigating puberty. Mason was only three years older. He'd been around a lot more and in the small town of Spirit Hollow, that meant everyone knew Willow was under his protection.

"So, what are you doing here?" she asked, pulling back from the warmth of him.

"Dad called me back," Mason answered, heaving a sigh that spoke volumes.

"Oh." Her brow scrunched up as she frowned, but then she caught the look in his eyes. "Ooooh," she drew the word out.

"I think he means it this time, Will. I'm not sure how to avoid it." He rubbed a hand over his face, his fingers pulling at scruff that covered his cheeks and chin. It was obvious that he hadn't shaved in at least a few days. Although, she recalled that as a wolf, he often had that constant five o'clock shadow going on.

"What did he say?" She asked, leaning back against the counter that she now stood in front of.

"He's calling a Moon Dance. He claims it's for the benefit of all unmated wolves, but I know it's because of me. He's been pushing for me to return for months. I don't know why it's become urgent, but he's not giving it up this time."

Willow's eyes widened in shock. A Moon Dance was a sacred tradition in the wolf shifter world. Mason had looped her in about it years before when the last one was called. He'd been just shy of twenty-five at the time and he'd left town rather than attending it. Other than a handful of visits over the last seven years, he'd stayed away. Willow wasn't even sure what exactly he'd been doing during that time.

"What are you going to do? Did you find a mate since your last visit?" she asked.

He shook his head, a grim look sliding over his features. "No. I wasn't exactly in a place to do much socializing. Plus, I'm pretty sure I don't have one."

Willow sighed. If she was a Cupid, she'd be able to tell him if his mate was nearby or not. But that wasn't her magic. "Maybe you could talk to my mom?" she suggested. "Or grandmother?"

Mason shook his head. "You know they don't ever answer questions outright. If I have a mate somewhere, they'll simply tell me to wait and she'll show up when the time is right or when I need her most or something like that."

She nodded. He was right. Although her mother and grandmother were Cupids, the way they *assisted* couples was not straightforward at all. She chuckled, thinking to herself before she spoke aloud. “Too bad you didn’t think to bring someone with you from outside. You could have pretended to have a mate and they’d have left you alone.”

www.ingramcontent.com/pod-product-compliance
Ingram Content Group UK Ltd.
Pitfield, Milton Keynes, MK11 3LW, UK
UKHW041641190726
13854UKWH00006B/2630

9 781698 395425